BY DOUG DUBOSQUE

PEEL
PRODUCTIONS

Published by Peel Productions, P.O. Box 185, Molalla, OR 97038.
Manufactured in the United States of America

1 3 5 7 9 8 4 3 2
First edition October 1993

Library of Congress Cataloging-in-Publication Data

DuBosque, D. C.
   Draw! Dinosaurs / by Doug DuBosque,
      p.   cm.
   Includes index
   ISBN 0-939217-20-1 (pbk.) : $8.95
   1. Dinosaurs in art--Juvenile literature. 2. Drawing--Technique-Juvenile
literature. [1. Dinosaurs in art. 2. Drawing-Technique.] I. Title.
   NC780.5.D83 1993
   736'.6--dc20   93-6091

CONTENTS

BEFORE YOU START...

YOU CAN DRAW WITH JUST ABOUT ANYTHING. People in caves used dried clay and black stuff out of the fire pit, and we're still talking about their drawings 25,000 years later! But caves, charcoal, mud and torches do not make for an optimal drawing environment. So find a comfortable place to draw – with decent light, so you can see what you're doing.

Draw with a pencil that's longer than your finger.

Find an eraser – not the one on your pencil, which will disappear quickly.

Plan to keep your drawings – you'll find instructions for a simple portfolio on page 80.

For paper, you might find "junk" paper to practice – backs of old photocopies and computer printouts work well. And the price is right!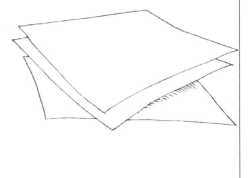

And don't forget to sharpen your pencil when it gets dull!

Most important, you need a **POSITIVE ATTITUDE. DO YOUR BEST!**

LINOSAURS

FOR AN EASY START,
DRAW ONE LINE AT A TIME.

CAMARASAURUS

Use a pencil.

Draw lightly at first.

Start with a long, swooping line.

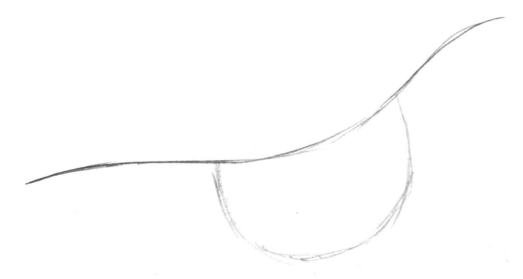

Then draw a curved line underneath it.

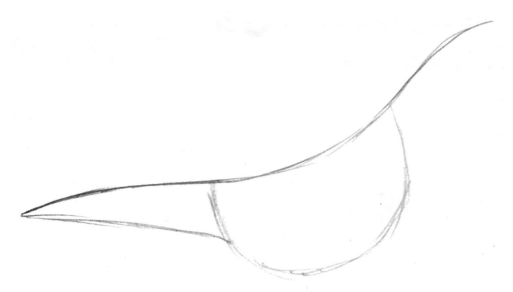

Add another line to make the a thick tail.

Always draw lightly at first!

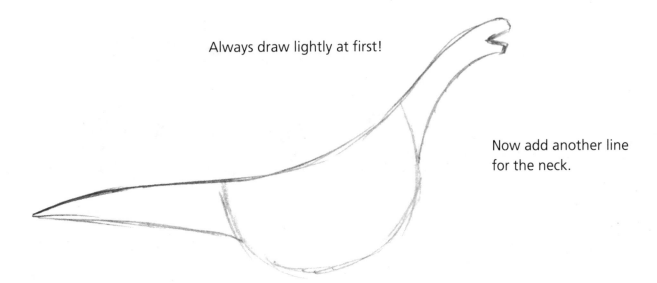

Now add another line
for the neck.

Draw the mouth. Try it again if it
doesn't look right the first time.

IF AT FIRST YOU DON'T SUCCEED...

Add legs...

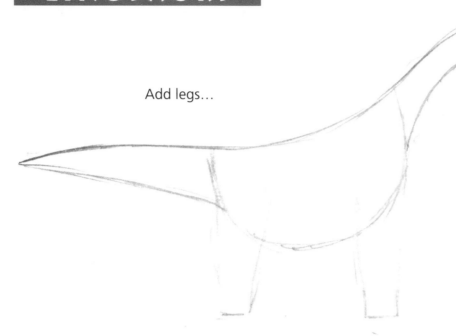

Where do the legs connect to the body?

...then eyes, nostrils and toe nails...

Now go over the lines you want to keep. You can erase the lines you don't need anymore.

CAMARASAURUS
Lived 140 million years ago (Jurassic.) Ate plants. 58 feet long (19 meters). Smaller than Brachiosaurus, but like Brachiosaurus has nostrils on top of head. Some people think it had a trunk like an elephant! (You can draw that if you want!)

(CAM-AR-A-SOR-US)

ALLOSAURUS

Start this drawing with a swooping line. Try to make it *just like* the one you see here.

Draw another line, down, and curving below the first.

Allosaurus has a big head and big jaws. Draw them with two boxes. It may take practice before you draw it exactly the way you want it.

...TRY, TRY AGAIN!

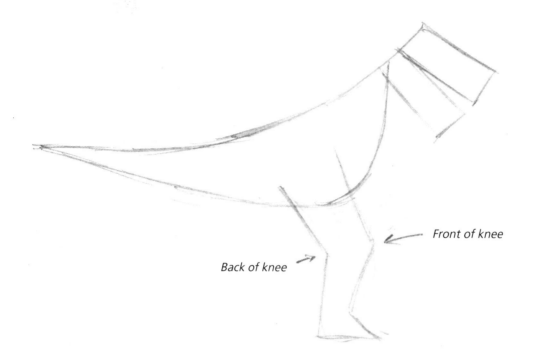

Front of knee

Back of knee

Next draw a leg. The leg looks complex, but actually it bends just the way your own leg bends, at the knee and at the ankle.

Make the other leg straight. Now your dinosaur looks as though it's walking!

With just a dot and a line, you can draw the eye.

Add teeth and arms.

Now go over the part you want to keep, and erase any parts you don't want.

But wait…!

Do you see some changes I've made in the final drawing?

ALLOSAURUS

Ate meat. Lived 145 million years ago (Jurassic). Up to 39 feet long (12 meters). Lived long before Tyrannosaurus Rex, and had longer arms with strong claws to hold its prey while it tore at it with teeth serrated like steak knives.

(AL-o-SOR-us)

STENONYCHOSAURUS

Start with a long, straight, *slanting* and *curving* line…

…with another curved line under it.

Add a bump on the back, plus lines for the tail and neck…

…and a box for the head.

Now add a leg, slightly bent. Notice that I draw this leg slanting towards the back, not straight up and down.

Also notice that the foot has a sickle claw that sticks up.

The second leg goes a little bit forward, and is slightly bent like the first leg.

The face is fairly easy…

…and the arms drop down, then bend forward, then end with two little sharp claws.

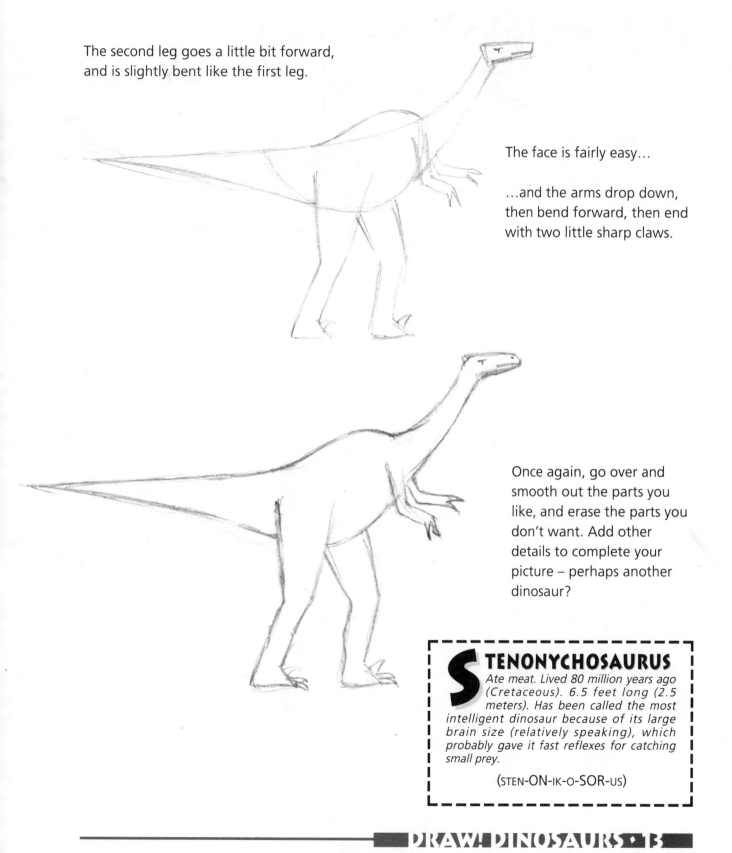

Once again, go over and smooth out the parts you like, and erase the parts you don't want. Add other details to complete your picture – perhaps another dinosaur?

STENONYCHOSAURUS

Ate meat. Lived 80 million years ago (Cretaceous). 6.5 feet long (2.5 meters). Has been called the most intelligent dinosaur because of its large brain size (relatively speaking), which probably gave it fast reflexes for catching small prey.

(STEN-ON-IK-O-SOR-US)

OURANOSAURUS

Start with a long. swooping line for the back…

…and add a curving line underneath.

Add two lines for the neck…

Pay special attention to the angle of the neck lines!

…and a line for the bottom of the tail.

Add a head. It's easy. The leg is more complicated. The bend in the ankle shows on both the front and the back of the leg.

This is different from the last dinosaur you drew!

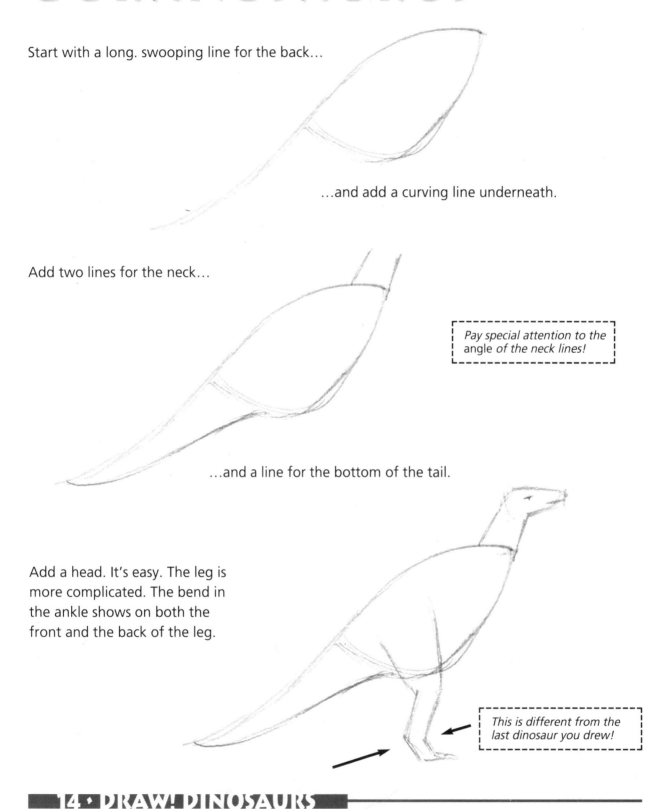

Now add three things:

1. Another leg;
2. Two arms with hands; and
3. The ridge on the back.

You might want to add more detail to the ridge of the back. As before, make the lines you want darker, and erase the ones you don't want.

OURANOSAURUS
Ate plants. Lived 105 million years ago (Cretaceous). 23 feet long (7 meters). Had a tall sail along its back, probably for regulating body temperature. Closely related to Iguanodon, and like it had spike-like thumbs.

(OO-RAN-O-SOR-US)

ANCHICERATOPS

It looks simple, but this drawing requires you to observe curves and shapes very carefully. Start with a curve for the back.

Then add a line for the bottom – look carefully!

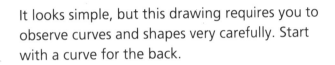

When you add the legs, notice how far back the front leg is. Also look how the legs bend toward each other.

Notice the position of the legs on the other side of the body. Draw them behind the others. As you draw the neck frill, look at how far back it extends – all the way to the front leg.

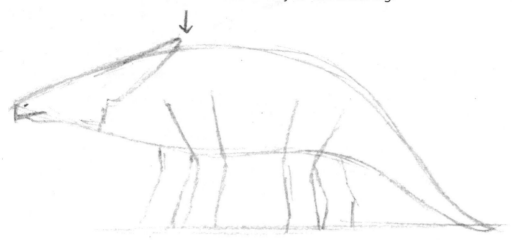

Anchiceratops has a small horn on its nose, and two long ones above the eye. Can you see how I draw one horn *behind* the other?

Anchiceratops also has little horns at the back edge of the frill on its neck.

Erase the lines you don't need. Make the good lines bolder. Add more details if you want to – wrinkles, plants....

ANCHICERATOPS
Ate plants. Lived 75 million years ago (Cretaceous). 20 feet long (6 meters). Had a long neck frill and one long horn above each eye, with a smaller one on the nose. The frill was probably for display, not for defense.

(AN-KI-CER-A-TOPS)

TUOJIANGOSAURUS

Start with two curving lines.

The beginning of this drawing looks a bit like a rug with something underneath it.!

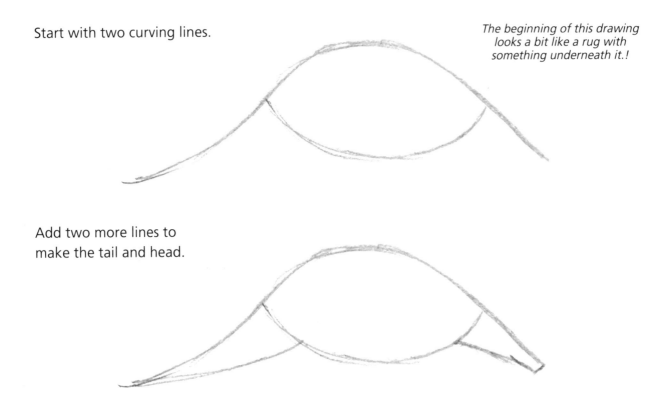

Add two more lines to make the tail and head.

Next add legs. The back legs are bigger and longer than the front. I've made a little "X" to show where each leg attaches to the rest of the skeleton.

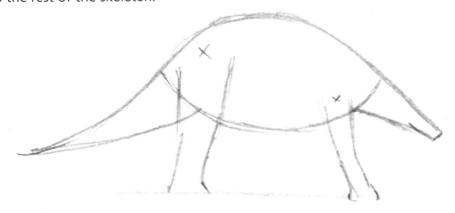

Add two more legs. Draw spikes on the tail and jagged bumps on the back.

(No one will attack this dinosaur!)

Don't forget the eye and mouth!

You might want to try adding a second row of plates on the back. Look carefully at how I draw them *behind* the first row.

Erase any lines you don't need in the final drawing.

Tuojiangosaurus

Ate plants, probably grazing like a horse. Lived 145 million years ago (Jurassic). 20 feet long (6 meters). Of all Stegosaurus-type skeletons found, this one, from China, is the best preserved.

(TWA-JAN-GO-SOR-US)

DSUNGARIPTERUS

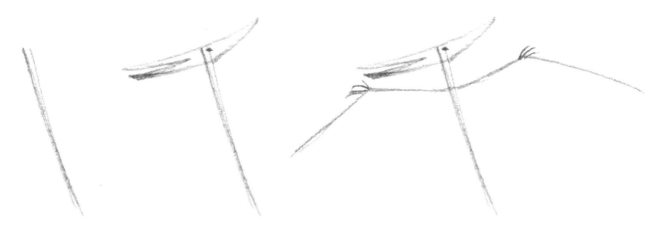

I think you'll have no problem drawing this creature…

…but can you pronounce its name?

Dsungaripterus was a type of *Pterosaur* (TER-o-sawr). Pterosaurs weren't actually dinosaurs, they were…

DSUNGARIPTERUS

Ate fish? Early Cretaceous (125 million years ago). Skull 16 inches long (41 centimeters). Unusual upward-curving beak – for eating shellfish and snails? Who knows?

(TSUN-GA-RIP-TER-US)

…flying reptiles.

OVALSAURS

FOR MORE FLEXIBILITY, BUILD FROM BASIC OVALS.

In this section, I'll show you one of my favorite techniques, which is starting lightly with ovals, and then adding parts to them.

OVALSAURS

In the first chapter, I showed you lines you can draw to make dinosaurs in one position. With those lines, it's hard to know how to draw dinosaurs in other positions.

To do that, you'll need to do what a cartoonist or animator would do: break the body into parts. Then, when you draw, you put each part where you want it, and finally blend them all together.

For example, here's a drawing you could copy fairly easily. You could draw it the same way, over and over and over. Which would be fine, if that's all you wanted to do.

But you'll be able to do much more with your drawing if you take the time to follow (and practice) the steps on the next few pages.

You'll be able to make your dinosaur look like it's walking...

...or reaching for leaves.

Or perhaps just trying to get a nap while baby Apatosaurs want to play.

STEP 1: DRAW AN OVAL

IMPORTANT!
Use a pencil for these drawings!

Draw it VERY lightly! It's easy to erase *light* lines. It's *not* easy to erase **dark** lines.

Think about your whole drawing right from the beginning. Leave enough room on your paper for the dinosaur's tail, neck, and legs.

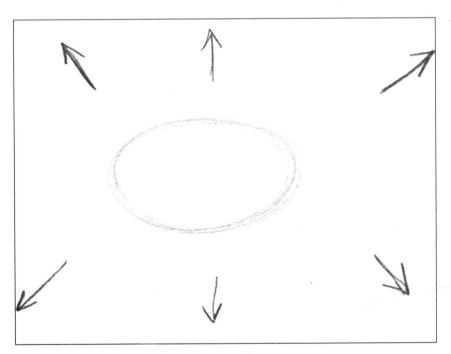

You don't want to run out of space on your paper!

STEP 2: ADD LEGS!

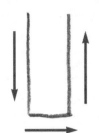

From the bottom of the oval, the legs are like little cylinders going to the ground. From the side, all you see is a line going down, across, and back up.

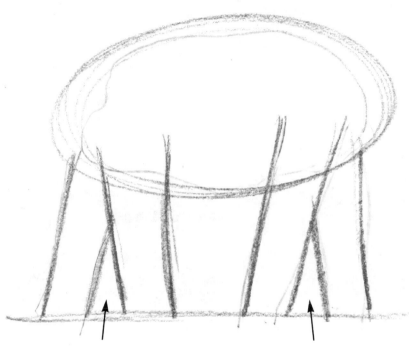

Pay special attention to the way the legs connect to the body. Make two of them appear behind the others.

Look at the shape *between* the legs – a triangle.

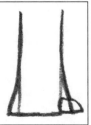

Want more detail? Make the foot a little wider at the bottom. And add toenails (of course).

STEP 3: ADD A TAIL!

The secret of drawing a great tail is to make it connect *smoothly* with the oval (the body).

The bottom part of the tail connects *smoothly* to the bottom part of the body.

The top part of the tail connects *smoothly* to the top of the body.

Make sure yours do!

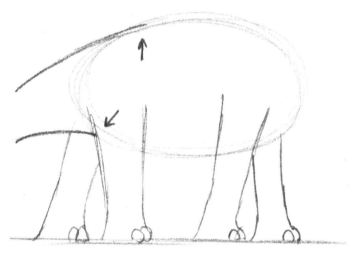

The arrows point to where the tail connects.

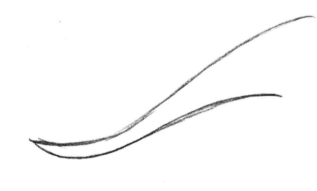

The top and the bottom get closer and closer together, until they meet in a point.

Do you want the tail to be straight? Or have a little curve? Or have a *lot* of curve?

It's your choice – it's your dinosaur!

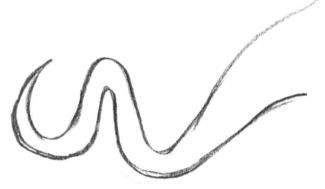

Have fun with your drawing! Who says dinosaur drawings have to be serious?

Here's a fancy, 3-D tail for you to try. It's not easy, but with a little practice you'll learn how to draw it.

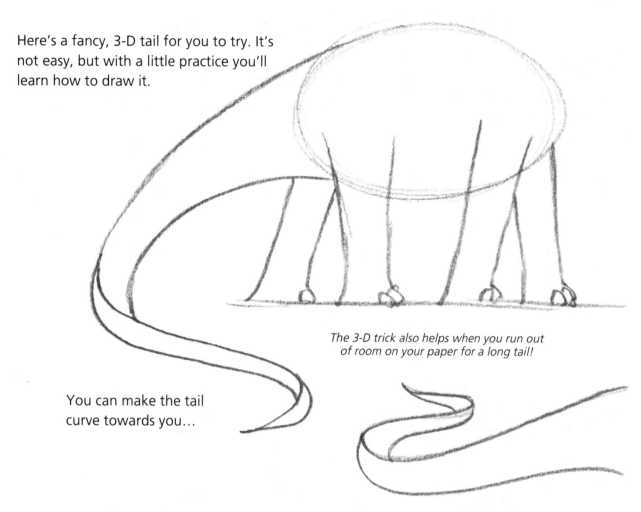

You can make the tail curve towards you…

The 3-D trick also helps when you run out of room on your paper for a long tail!

…or you can make it go away from you!

"How do you draw that?" you ask. The key is to look very carefully at the lines, then practice, then look some more. Pay special attention to where lines connect together!

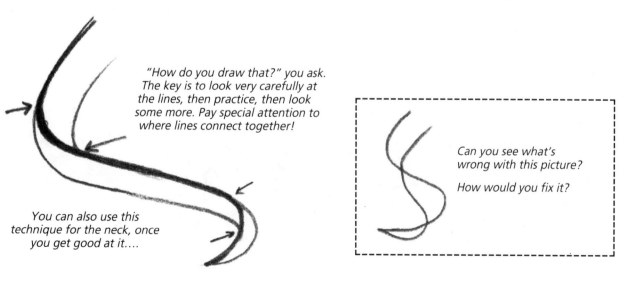

You can also use this technique for the neck, once you get good at it….

Can you see what's wrong with this picture?

How would you fix it?

STEP 4: ADD A HEAD

When you place the head in your drawing, be sure to leave plenty of room for the neck.

Start out very lightly with a circle.

Add a box shape for the nose and mouth.

Make an eye with a dot and a curved line above it (you only see one eye from the side). Then add mouth, nostrils, and ear holes....

STEP 5: ADD A NECK!

With ovalsaurs, you can draw the same *character* – not just the same *drawing* – over and over again. When you draw a *character,* think about how your character moves and behaves, what it likes and doesn't like.

For example, your dinosaur probably doesn't like having a neck that looks like a stick, so this would not be a happy dinosaur!

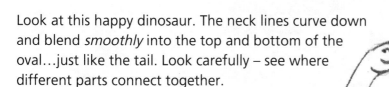

Look at this happy dinosaur. The neck lines curve down and blend *smoothly* into the top and bottom of the oval...just like the tail. Look carefully – see where different parts connect together.

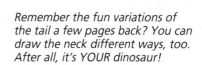

Remember the fun variations of the tail a few pages back? You can draw the neck different ways, too. After all, it's YOUR dinosaur!

940476

STEP 6: ADMIRE YOUR CREATION!

Erase the lines you don't want, add a few wrinkles and shadows (or colors!) and your drawing is done.

Here's what I like about this technique: when you draw by putting pieces together, you can easily change the position of your dinosaur.

A PATOSAURUS

Lived 145 million years ago (Jurassic). Ate plants. 69 feet long (21 meters). One of the best-known dinosaurs. Has also been called "Brontosaurus."

(A-PAT-O-SOR-us)

Try drawing these variations, starting with an oval and adding pieces to it.

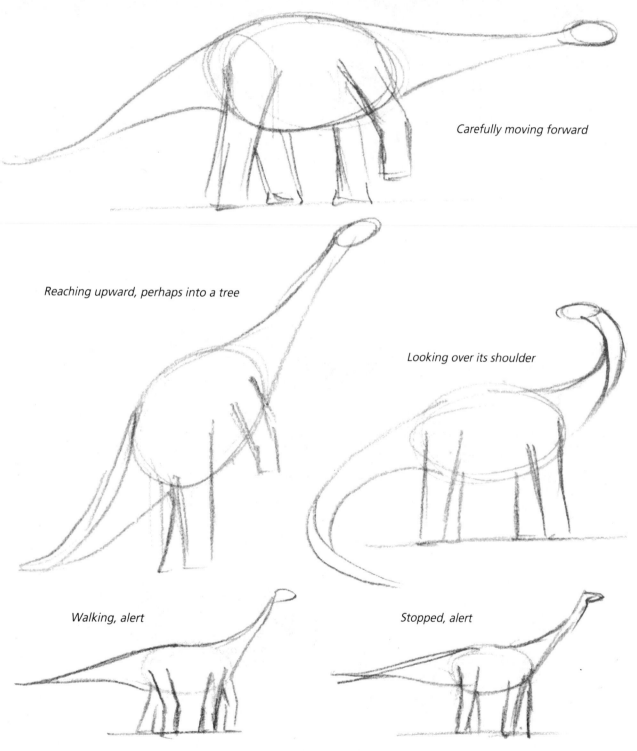

Carefully moving forward

Reaching upward, perhaps into a tree

Looking over its shoulder

Walking, alert

Stopped, alert

How are the legs different in these two drawings?

PARASAUROLOPHUS

Let's draw another very distinctive dinosaur, one of the hadrosaurs.

Start with an oval. Draw lightly. Make one end higher than the other. (You don't need to draw the line in the middle.)

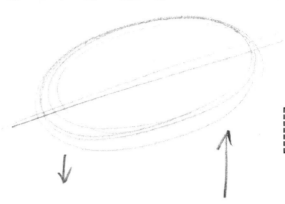

> One end of the oval is higher!

Add legs – large ones in the back and quite small ones in the front.

Crest on head

Ridge on back

Draw a neck, head, crest on the head, tail, and maybe just a little bit of a ridge along the back.

Add a little bit of shading, and you're well on your way to having a Parasaurolophus.

This is a dinosaur that's easier to draw than pronounce.

By changing the position of the first oval , the legs and tail, you can make it standing up. What other Parasaurolophus positions can you draw?

PARASAUROLOPHUS Lived 70 million years ago (Cretaceous). Ate plants. 33 feet long (10 meters). The long crest on its head was probably a visual signal to other dinosaurs. It might have supported brightly colored skin connected to the neck, like a flag or banner. It wasn't *a snorkel!*

(PAR-A-SOR-O-LO-FUS)

ANKYLOSAURUS

Start with an oval, add legs, tapering neck and tail with ovals on the end...

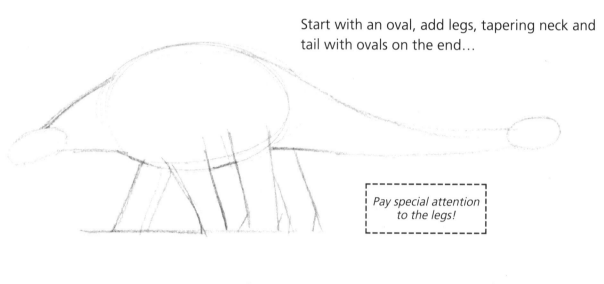

Pay special attention to the legs!

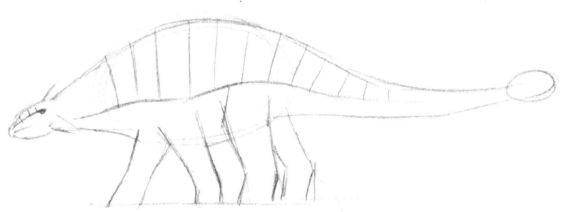

...then some ridges on the back and bumps, and you have an Ankylosaurus.

Add wrinkles, textures, shading and shadows. The more time you spend on your drawing, the better it will look!

Using its tail as a weapon

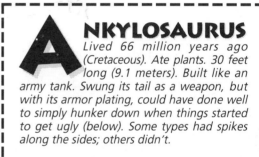

ANKYLOSAURUS

ANKYLOSAURUS
Lived 66 million years ago (Cretaceous). Ate plants. 30 feet long (9.1 meters). Built like an army tank. Swung its tail as a weapon, but with its armor plating, could have done well to simply hunker down when things started to get ugly (below). Some types had spikes along the sides; others didn't.

(AN-KY-LO-SOR-US)

Trying NOT to become someone's lunch!

PACHYCEPHALOSAURUS

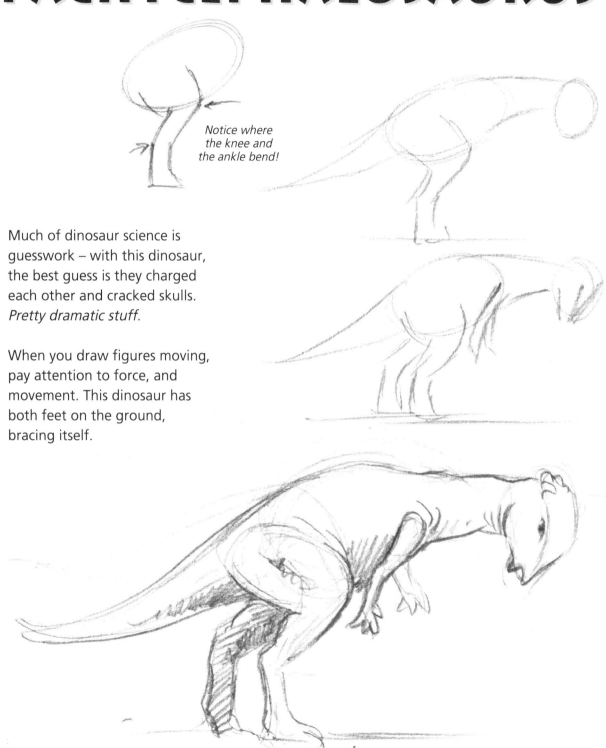

Notice where the knee and the ankle bend!

Much of dinosaur science is guesswork – with this dinosaur, the best guess is they charged each other and cracked skulls. *Pretty dramatic stuff.*

When you draw figures moving, pay attention to force, and movement. This dinosaur has both feet on the ground, bracing itself.

This dinosaur is charging, so the first oval I draw is tilted forward. One leg is in the air.

PACHYCEPHALOSAURUS
Lived 65 million years ago (Cretaceous). Ate plants. 26 feet long (8 meters). Scientists have decided that the extraordinarily thick skulls served as crash helmets, and that male dinosaurs would butt heads to establish dominance, as males of some species still do today.

(PAK-EE-SEF-o-LO-SOR-us)

Are either of these dinosaurs *balanced?* No, instead each looks like it's about to fall over in the direction of the other, so that they could easily be about to collide – exactly the way I want the drawing to look.

STEGOSAURUS

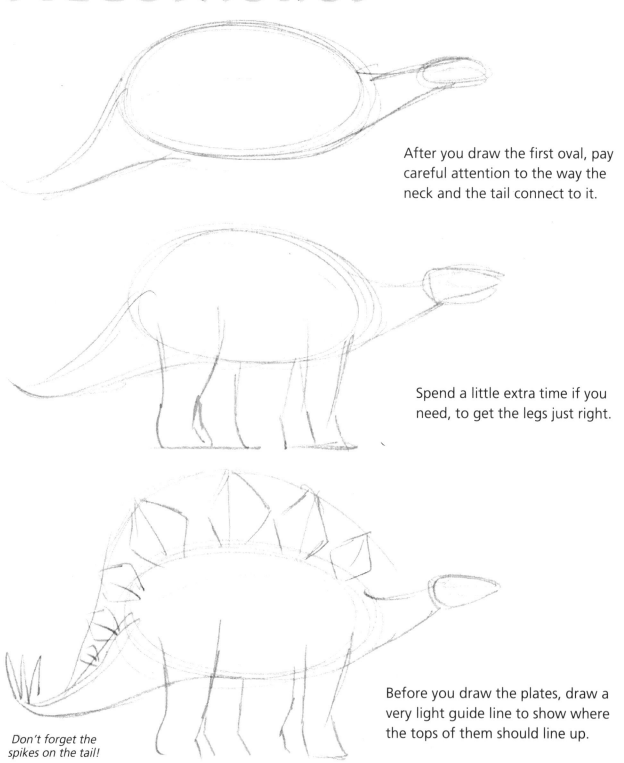

After you draw the first oval, pay careful attention to the way the neck and the tail connect to it.

Spend a little extra time if you need, to get the legs just right.

Before you draw the plates, draw a very light guide line to show where the tops of them should line up.

Don't forget the spikes on the tail!

As you finish your drawing, you might wonder, as I do, what colors dinosaurs really were.

Did *Stegosaurus* have a camouflage pattern?

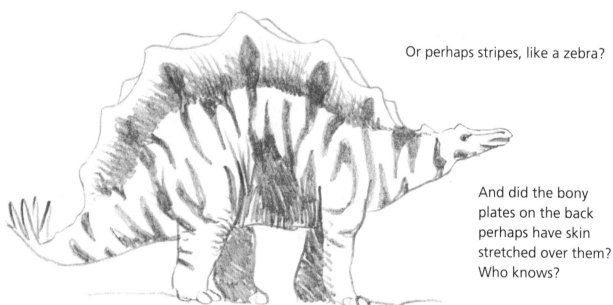

Or perhaps stripes, like a zebra?

And did the bony plates on the back perhaps have skin stretched over them? Who knows?

STEGOSAURUS
Lived 145 million years ago (Jurassic). Ate plants. 22 feet long (6.7 meters). Spikes on end of tail for defense. Scientists still debate position function of those big plates on the back.

(STEG-o-SOR-us)

KENTROSAURUS

This is similar to the drawing on the last two pages, but there are some important differences I want you to notice.

First, notice how the oval tilts toward the front of the dinosaur – you don't have to draw the line, but do look at it!

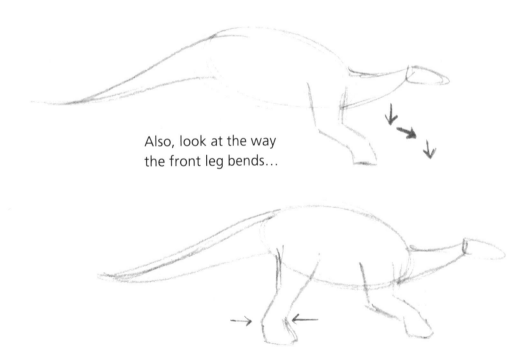

Second, notice that the *bottom* of the tail is at a level with the *top* of the neck.

Also, look at the way the front leg bends…

…and the rear leg as well.

It looks like the spikes on the back should be real easy to draw – and they are. Even so, notice how I carefully sketch them in *lightly* first, just to be sure they're right before I **darken** them.

Kentrosaurus has a spike sticking out sideways from the hip. A little bit of shadow underneath makes it more realistic.

KENTROSAURUS
Lived 145 million years ago (Jurassic). Ate plants. 10 feet long (3 meters). Stegosaurus-like plates become spikes farther back. Extra spikes stuck out sideways from the hip.

(KEN-TRO-SOR-US)

MAIASAURA

Once again, we start with an oval. Is it level, or does it tilt slightly toward one side?

As with the *Kentrosaurus,* look carefully at where the *bottom* of the tail and the *top* of the neck connect to the oval.

The "good mother reptile" is going to be tending eggs in a nest, so her back leg is bent. The curve of the calf (lower leg) is also a key line to pay attention to.

The arms bend just like a person's arms. The nest is just a few lines. How much of each egg can you actually see in the drawing?

MAIASAURA

Ate plants. 29 feet long (9 meters). Name means "good mother reptile" – because of the discovery in 1978 of fossilized baby Maiasaura and eggs around a mound-shaped nest in Montana, the first evidence of dinosaurs with organized family structure.

(MY-A-SOR-A)

PLESIOSAURUS

Having problems drawing dinosaur legs? Try drawing a Plesiosaurus swimming. It's easy!

P **LESIOSAURUS**
*6-28 feet long (2-9 meters).
Swam by flapping front flippers
up and down. Probably moved
its neck very quickly to catch fish. Alas, not a
dinosaur but a swimming reptile.*

(PLEES-EE-O-SOR-US)

TRIANGLESAURS

SOMETIMES, OTHER
SHAPES WILL JUMP OUT
AT YOU. DRAW THEM!

Beyond drawing lines and ovals, one of the most
helpful tricks I know is to try to divide your
subject into triangles.

Like lines and ovals, triangles give you one more
way of looking – and a better chance to get your
drawing right on the first try.

BRACHIOSAURUS

Look at the drawing above.

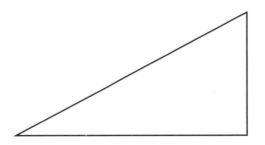

Do you see a triangle?

Look at *just* the dinosaur.

You might see a BIG triangle…

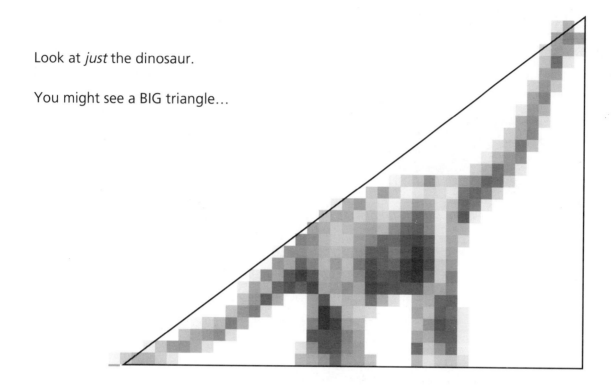

…or a smaller triangle.

Either one can give you a good start for your drawing. Since the neck is fairly easy to draw, I think I'd prefer the smaller triangle.

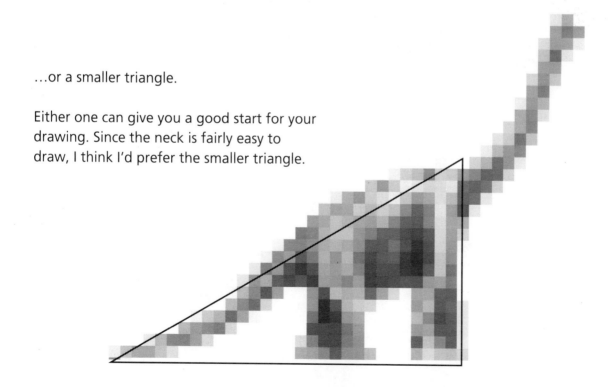

TRIANGLESAURS

Look carefully at the shape, and each of the angles of the triangle, before you draw it.

Start out lightly with the triangle. Stop drawing and make sure it looks right before you go on.

Next add a light curving line for the neck.

Draw a face, then another line for the bottom of the neck.

Look again at the original drawing, and you'll see that the back of the dinosaur is not a straight line. You need to add curves to it.

Add curves – lightly! Keep looking back and forth between your drawing and the original. Where's the middle of the triangle's top side? Where does the curved line cross it?

Observe carefully as you add legs – notice how the legs closest to you block your view of part of the legs on the other side.

The next step of the drawing will be to add shadow, then details.

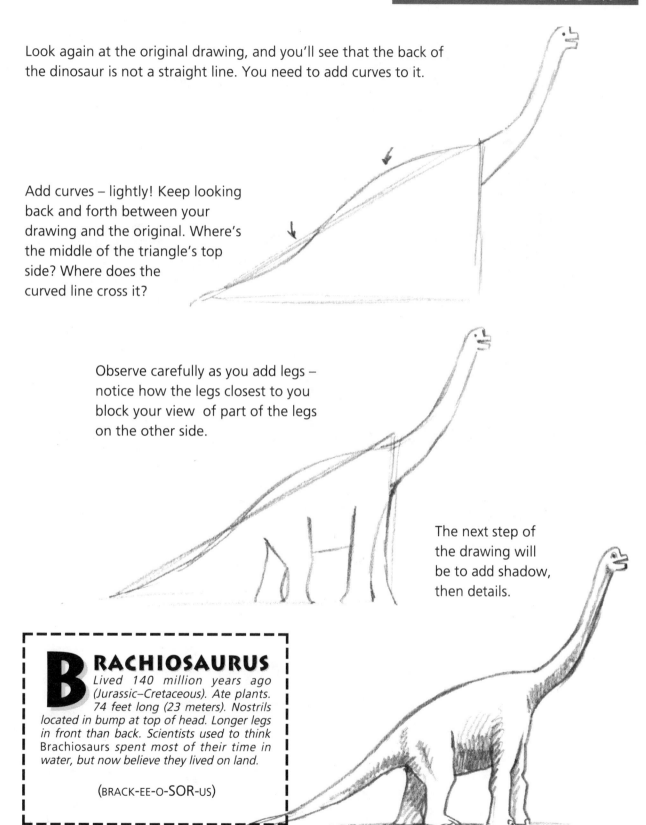

BRACHIOSAURUS

Lived 140 million years ago (Jurassic–Cretaceous). Ate plants. 74 feet long (23 meters). Nostrils located in bump at top of head. Longer legs in front than back. Scientists used to think Brachiosaurs spent most of their time in water, but now believe they lived on land.

(BRACK-EE-O-SOR-US)

TYRANNOSAURUS REX

The best-known dinosaur of all can be a difficult one to draw.

We'll start by looking for triangles.

Look at just the shapes of the dinosaur itself.

Do you see the triangle I see?

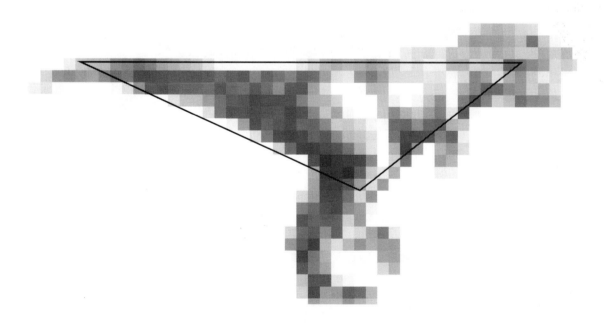

TRIANGLESAURS

Start with a triangle…

Remember, any time your drawing starts having a problem,

1) Stop.

2) Look.

3) Listen.

(Really! Talk to yourself, out loud if you need to, about what's wrong with your drawing. As if you were someone else, trying to help you make it better. And listen for any helpful advice.)

…add a box for the head…

…plus an arm and a tail…

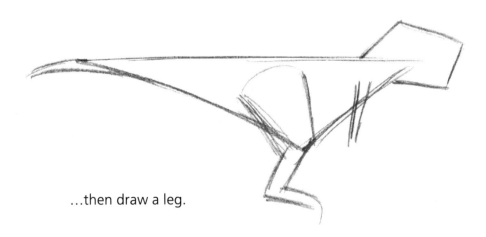

…then draw a leg.

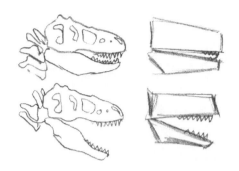

When you draw the head, think of it as two boxes. The bottom box (the jaw) is smaller than the top box.

You can draw the eyes with a few curved lines.

Add another leg…

…and then keep going with details and shading.

TYRANNOSAURUS REX

Lived 65 million years ago (Cretaceous, not Jurassic). Ate meat. Lots of it. 46 feet long (14 meters). Probably waited in ambush, then chased its prey for a fairly short distance. Slammed into it with open jaws, swung it about violently, and swallowed large chunks whole. Yum! Very short arms were probably just used to arise from sleeping position.

(TIE-RAN-O-SOR-US WRECKS)

VELOCIRAPTOR

As you pick out shapes in this drawing of *Velociraptor,* you'll probably
see that there are many different ways you can attack the drawing....

You can see the body as being one big triangle, and start your drawing with that triangle....

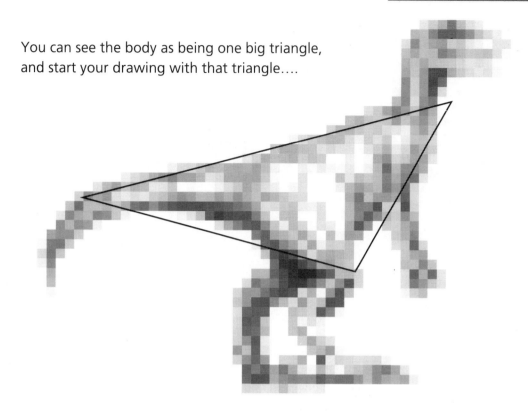

Or you might see a more complicated shape that you think would be a good place to start. Generally, it's best to start with the simplest shapes you can find, and then draw them as accurately as you can.

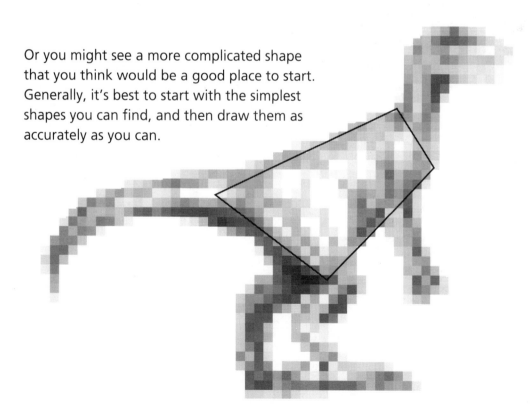

TRIANGLESAURS

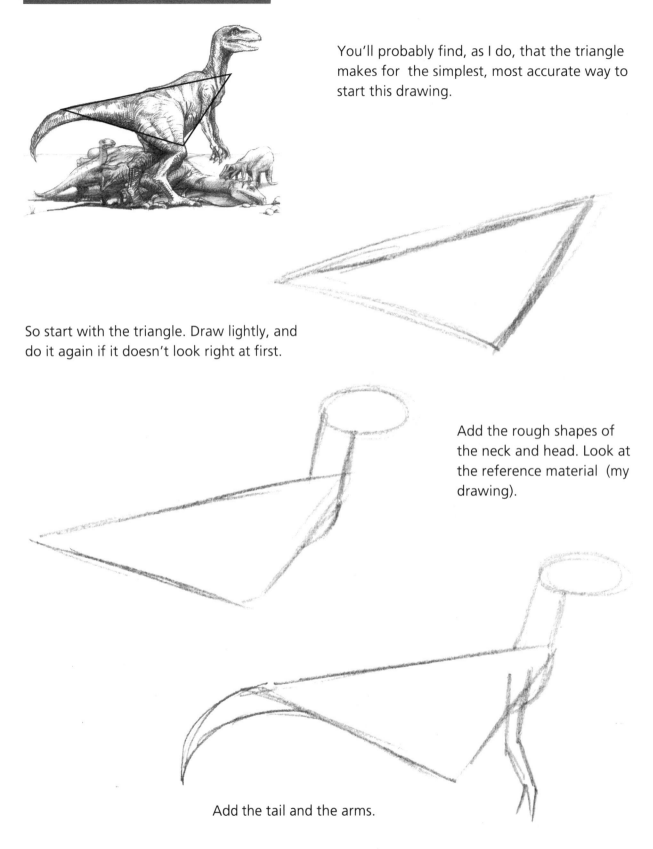

You'll probably find, as I do, that the triangle makes for the simplest, most accurate way to start this drawing.

So start with the triangle. Draw lightly, and do it again if it doesn't look right at first.

Add the rough shapes of the neck and head. Look at the reference material (my drawing).

Add the tail and the arms.

The legs are more complicated. Can you see how the top part of the leg forms part of a triangle?

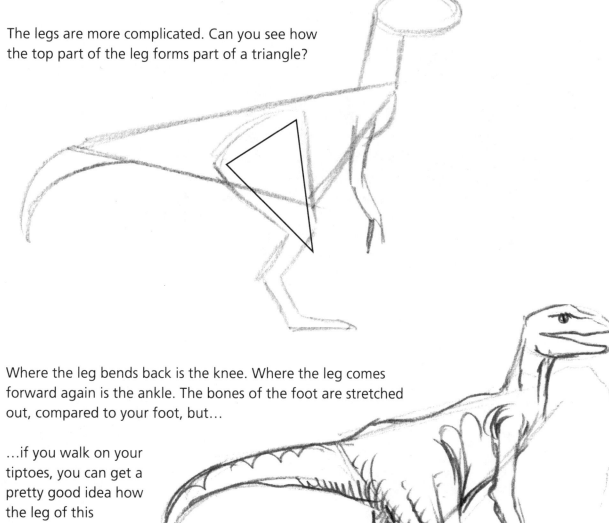

Where the leg bends back is the knee. Where the leg comes forward again is the ankle. The bones of the foot are stretched out, compared to your foot, but…

…if you walk on your tiptoes, you can get a pretty good idea how the leg of this dinosaur worked.

Ankles

Knee

VELOCIRAPTOR
Lived 75 million years ago (Cretaceous). Ate meat. 6 feet long (1.8 meters). Probably hunted in packs, attacking with claws and teeth. Not as big as the movie version!

(VEL-OS-I-RAP-TOR)

STEGOSAURUS

I showed you how to draw Stegosaurus earlier with ovals, and how to draw its cousin Tuojiangosaurus with lines. It's one of my favorites. Let's look at it one more time, but this time let's look for triangles.

How many triangles do you see?

I find two…

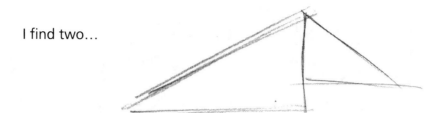

…perhaps you see others that would help you start your drawing.

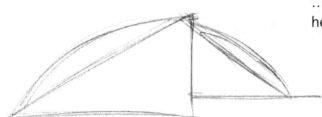

There are no rules to this type of drawing. Just keep looking until you find something – whether a line, an oval, or a triangle – that helps you get your drawing started.

PTERANODON

There's no "right" and "wrong" to using triangles, lines or ovals when you draw. Much of drawing is simply seeing. As you get in the habit of looking for lines, ovals, and triangles, you'll be surprised how much more you see – and amazed how much more you can draw!

Use whatever approach works best for you with the drawing you're trying to do.

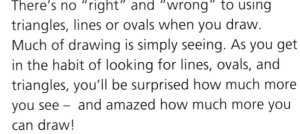

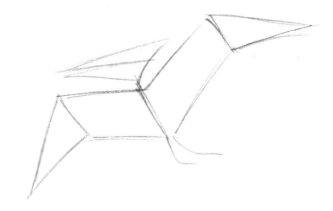

PTERANODON
Lived 70 million years ago (late Cretaceous). Long, toothless jaw was counterbalanced by bony crest at top of head. Probably scooped fish out of the ocean, as pelicans do today – and probably had a pelican-like pouch as well.

(TER-AN-O-DON)

SOLIDSAURS

FOR MAXIMUM EFFECT, TRY BUILDING FORMS AS YOU DRAW.

What you'll see in the next few pages will show you how basic forms can be combined to make a drawing that looks like a real, solid object. Drawing "solidsaurs" may not come naturally to you. Until you understand the basic forms, you might find this material difficult to draw.

I don't find this material difficult now. It comes quite easily to me....but guess what? I've been looking and drawing for *years*. Do you think there's a connection between years of practice and being good at something?

If you find this material difficult, keep looking and drawing. It will get easier!

Here are some basic shapes: an oval, a rectangle…

…and here they are as basic FORMS: a balloon (or egg), and a cylinder.
Can you draw them?

Here are variations of the cylinder.
Can you draw them? (Do it!)

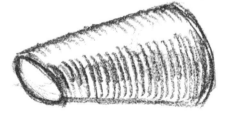

Notice how I draw contour lines wrapping around each object to help make it look more rounded?

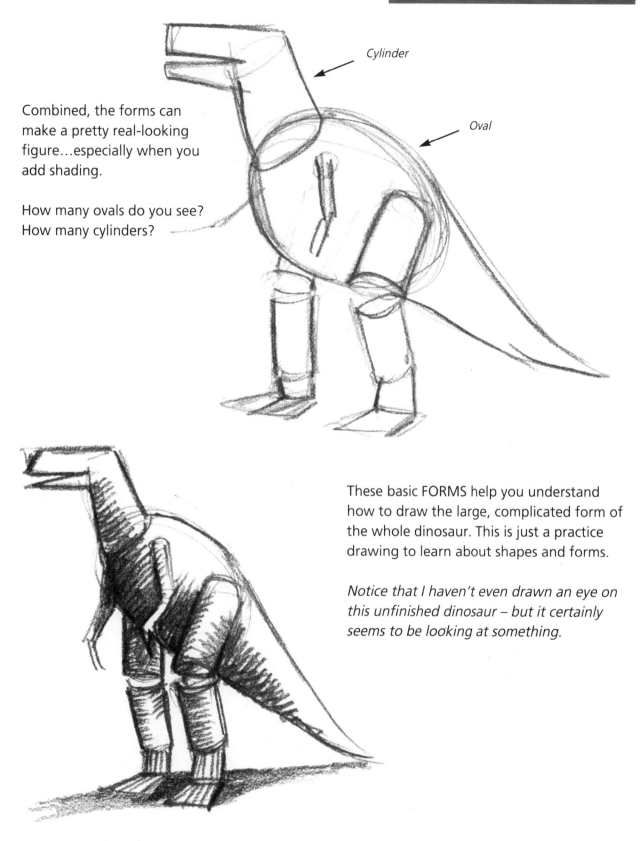

Cylinder

Oval

Combined, the forms can make a pretty real-looking figure...especially when you add shading.

How many ovals do you see? How many cylinders?

These basic FORMS help you understand how to draw the large, complicated form of the whole dinosaur. This is just a practice drawing to learn about shapes and forms.

Notice that I haven't even drawn an eye on this unfinished dinosaur – but it certainly seems to be looking at something.

Let's look at the forms that make up the dinosaur's leg. Here are a rectangle (or a cylinder from the side) and two views of a cylinder that has a line in the middle. Can you draw them? (Do it! It's important!)

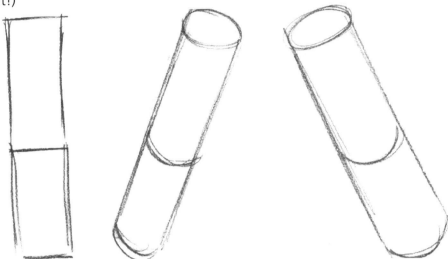

Now let's "break" the cylinder. There's an important difference between A and B. Do you see it?

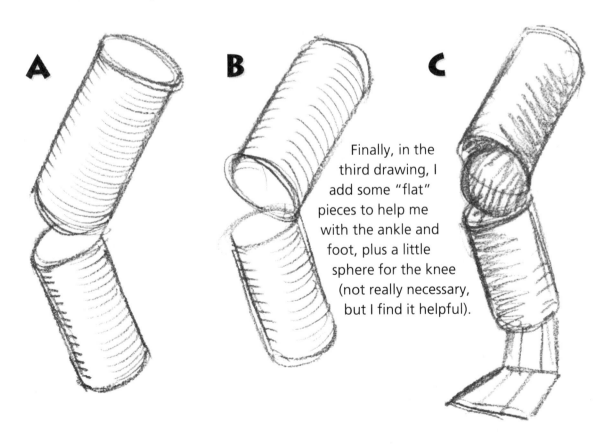

A

B

C

Finally, in the third drawing, I add some "flat" pieces to help me with the ankle and foot, plus a little sphere for the knee (not really necessary, but I find it helpful).

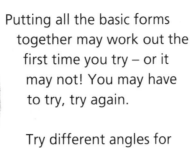

Putting all the basic forms together may work out the first time you try – or it may not! You may have to try, try again.

Try different angles for the legs.

The animators who created the dinosaurs in the movie *Jurassic Park* took acting classes and pretended they were dinosaurs. Can you move like you're a dinosaur?

It might help your drawing!

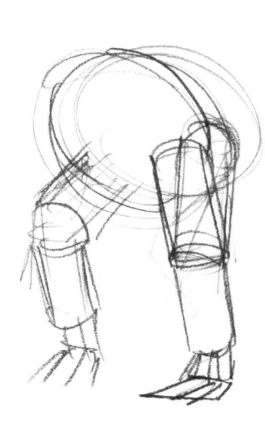

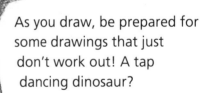

As you draw, be prepared for some drawings that just don't work out! A tap dancing dinosaur?

Make a note of it – you may need a tap-dancing dinosaur drawing as a reference some day!

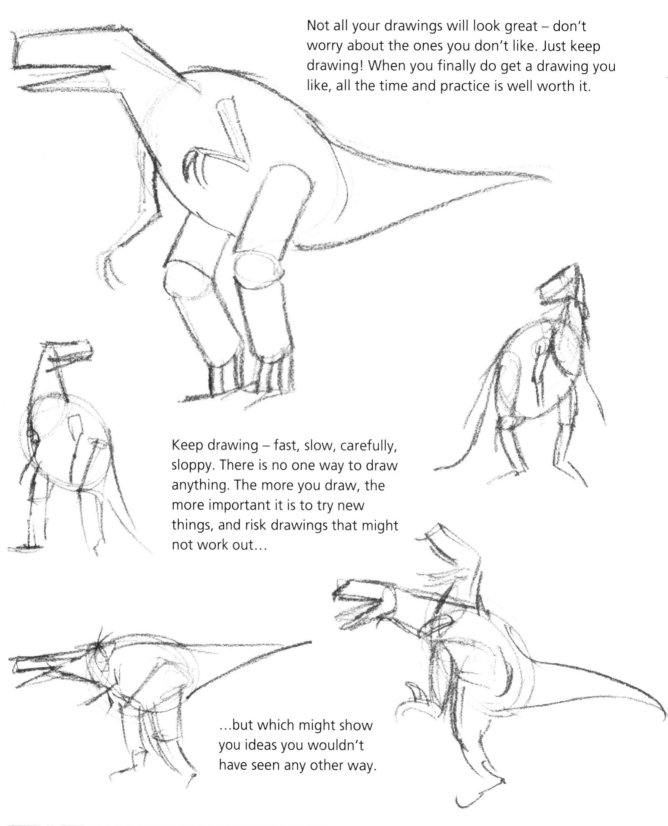

Not all your drawings will look great – don't worry about the ones you don't like. Just keep drawing! When you finally do get a drawing you like, all the time and practice is well worth it.

Keep drawing – fast, slow, carefully, sloppy. There is no one way to draw anything. The more you draw, the more important it is to try new things, and risk drawings that might not work out…

…but which might show you ideas you wouldn't have seen any other way.

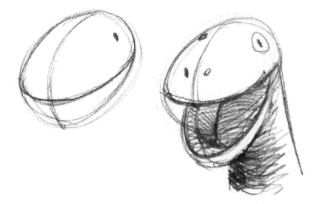

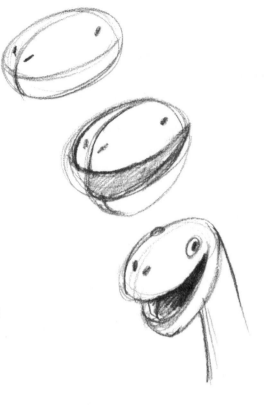

Also, take time to play with goofy ideas.

Believe it or not, these goofy-looking dinosaur heads can help you draw more realistic dinosaur heads. You can draw them – maybe not the first time. Keep looking, and you'll see how I drew these.

As you become more comfortable drawing solidsaurs, even goofy-looking ones, you might want to invent your own cartoon dinosaur character....

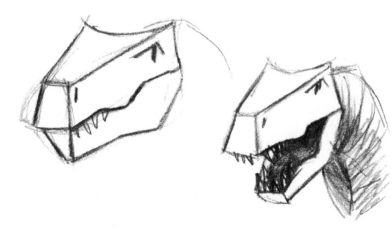

Your cartoon dinosaur character doesn't have to follow real dinosaur rules. It's *your* dinosaur. Make it in any position you want.

The best part of solidsaurs is that by combining basic forms you can make your dinosaur look like a real, solid character.

With enough practice and patience, you could even make an animated cartoon with your character – !

Have fun with your drawing!

MORE DINOSAURS

GAIN INSIGHT AND IDEAS FROM DRAWINGS IN PROGRESS

In this last section, I want to share with you some of the thoughts I have as I draw. Many of the drawings that follow are based on pictures by other artists. Their illustrations may show the knowledge they have of certain dinosaurs, so by looking closely at their work I can learn from their pictures. Of course, it would be great if they were here to guide me, but…

…they're not! So I have to guide myself.

I don't use other artists' work for reference material often, but with dinosaurs, that's all there is. You won't find many real dinosaurs, or photos of real dinosaurs (though the dinosaurs in *Jurassic Park* come pretty close!).

SCELIDOSAURUS

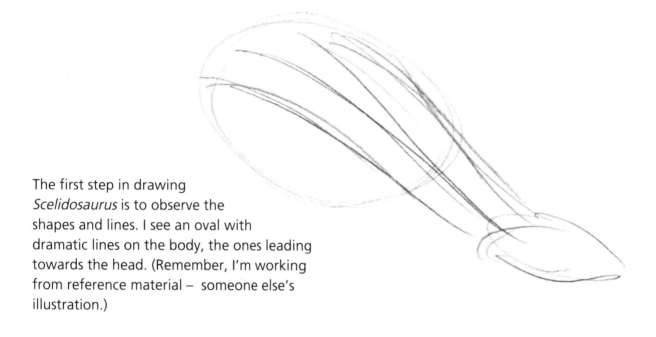

The first step in drawing *Scelidosaurus* is to observe the shapes and lines. I see an oval with dramatic lines on the body, the ones leading towards the head. (Remember, I'm working from reference material – someone else's illustration.)

Next comes careful observation of the tail and legs. They must be positioned just right, which means looking very closely at the angles formed by lines as they connect.

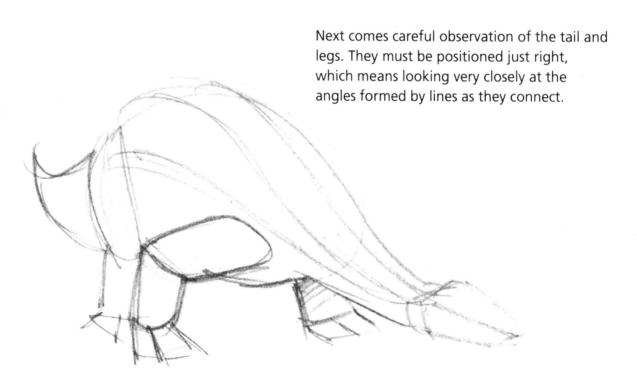

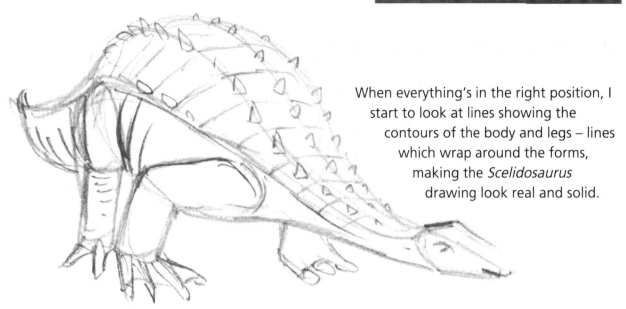

When everything's in the right position, I start to look at lines showing the contours of the body and legs – lines which wrap around the forms, making the *Scelidosaurus* drawing look real and solid.

SCELIDOSAURUS
Lived 185 million years ago (Jurassic). Ate plants. 13 feet long (4 meters). Probably a slow-moving dinosaur, it had very sturdy legs and bony knobs on its back. It's one of the few dinosaurs where fossils show an impression of the skin!

(SKEL-IDE-O-SOR-US)

You can see that the final drawing involves quite a bit of time, refining shadows, adding texture (with little lines and circles on the back), and sketching in some vegetation.

SEGNOSAURUS

I like an illustration I found of *Segnosaur* because of its pose – as though it has just spotted something on the shore after catching a fish.

My first step in drawing it is to figure out the main shapes of the body; the torso, neck and head…

…and then the legs.

The leg in the air presents the challenge of *foreshortening* – making something in the drawing look like it's coming toward you, or going away from you. The arms also come toward you in this drawing, but somehow they don't seem to be as much a challenge as that one leg.

Since I'm working from an existing illustration, I look back to it for any unusual angles and subtleties I might not have noticed before.

You can see that my attention is very much on that raised leg – trying to figure how to add to the foreshortening with contour lines wrapping around the upper leg, and with a shadow on the lower leg.

Notice the foreshortening: on the dinosaur's right leg (the straight one), the knee is behind the left wrist, the ankle just above the water. Contrast that with the raised leg, where the ankle is almost directly behind the knee – you hardly see any of the part of the leg that is foreshortened.

SEGNOSAURUS
(Cretaceous). 20 feet long (6 meters).This drawing is actually a hypothetical "segnosaur," depicting the best guess so far, which is that these dinosaurs fed on fish.

(SEG-NO-SAW-RUS)

DIENONYCHUS

Looking at my reference material (another artist's illustration), I start by roughly sketching the shape of the head and body.

Next I note positions of arms and legs.

It seems to me that something isn't quite right with my drawing. Somehow it doesn't look as fierce as I want it to. I start thinking about lines that would "wrap around" parts of the body, following contours – to give it greater depth.

To accentuate the texture of the skin, I add felt pen to my pencil drawing, being careful to keep *light* parts *light* while making shadows even **darker.**

Still, it doesn't seem very convincing to me. The pose – the way the dinosaur is positioned – just seems silly. It seems like it's dancing a jig, rather than attacking.

Finally, I decide this drawing isn't going anywhere, so I put it away (notice I don't *throw* it away) and start working on something else.

*(The problem turns out to be this: in the original illustration, my reference material, there's a much larger dinosaur **behind** this dinosaur – no wonder this one looks funny by itself!)*

DIENONYCHUS
Lived 105 million years ago (Cretaceous). Ate meat. 10 feet long (3 meters). Probably hunted in packs, attacking with claws and teeth. This would be a dinosaur to steer clear of!

(DIE-NO-**NIKE**-US)

ATTACK!

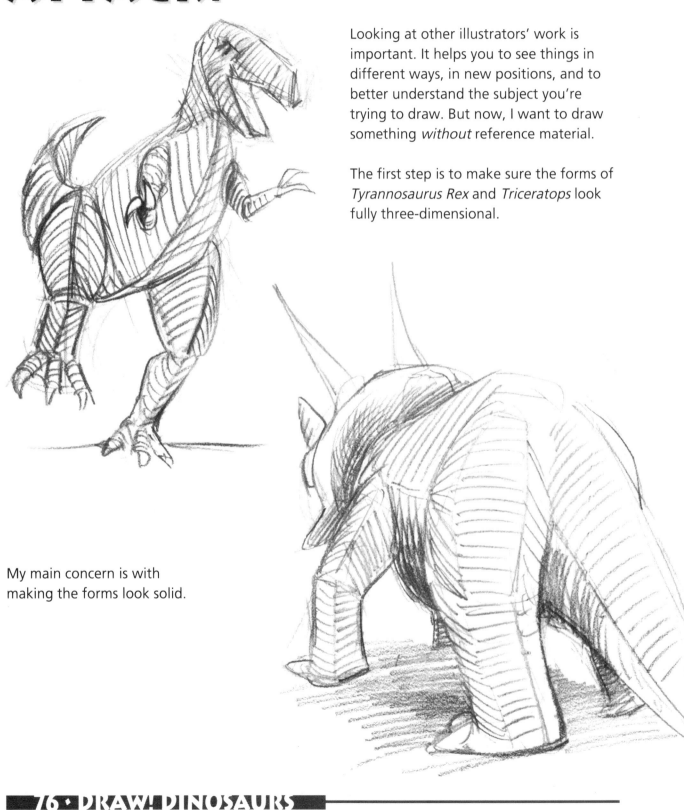

Looking at other illustrators' work is important. It helps you to see things in different ways, in new positions, and to better understand the subject you're trying to draw. But now, I want to draw something *without* reference material.

The first step is to make sure the forms of *Tyrannosaurus Rex* and *Triceratops* look fully three-dimensional.

My main concern is with making the forms look solid.

The next step makes them look a bit like stuffed animals. You still see contour lines, but *T. Rex* gains depth as I add shadows.

These are just studies, not final drawings. One thing I might change in the final drawing is the proportions of legs and arms, which are too big to be scientifically accurate. But if I want to make a cartoon or use the drawings some other way, these studies might be perfect just as they are.

I save these studies in my portfolio, for future reference.

BEFORE YOU QUIT...

1. REMEMBER THIS

One of the great secrets of our world is that behind every success there's always plenty of practice. The people who do amazing feats of daring, skill, or ingenuity have been practicing, often for much longer than you'd imagine. They've probably failed more often than you can imagine, too, so don't waste time being discouraged. If your drawings don't look exactly the way you'd like them to (especially the first try), **stop, look, listen, and try again!**

2. SAVE YOUR DRAWINGS!

Whenever you do a drawing—or even a sketch—put your initials (or autograph!) and date on it. And save it. You don't have to save it until it turns yellow and crumbles to dust, but do keep your drawings, at least for several months. Sometimes, hiding in your portfolio, they will mysteriously improve! I've seen it happen often with my own drawings, especially the ones I *knew* were no good at all, but kept anyway....

If you don't have your own portfolio, here's a way to make one inexpensively (you can find a fancy one at an art supply store if you'd rather):

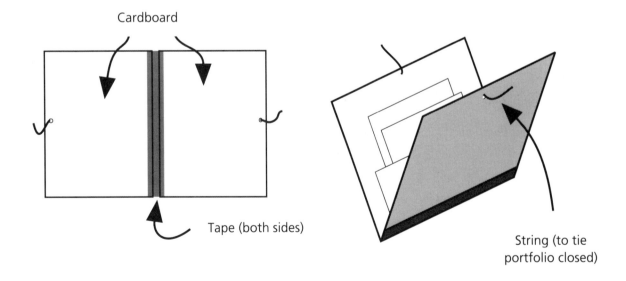

Cardboard

Tape (both sides)

String (to tie portfolio closed)

INDEX